Slip the Otter
Finds a Home

Written and Illustrated by Olena Kassian

Consultant, Dr. Thomas D. Nudds, Dept. of Zoology, University of Guelph

 An OWL Magazine/GOLDEN PRESS® Book

Text and art copyright© 1984 by Olena Kassian. All rights reserved. Printed in the U.S.A. by Western Publishing Company, Inc. OWL Magazine is a trademark of the Young Naturalist Foundation. GOLDEN® & Design, A GOLDEN LOOK-LOOK® BOOK and GOLDEN PRESS® are trademarks of Western Publishing Company, Inc. No part of this book may be reproduced or copied in any form without written permission from the publisher. Library of Congress Catalog Card Number: 83-83286
Canadian ISBN 0-919872-90-5
U.S. ISBN 0-307-12475-4 / ISBN 0-307-62475-7 (lib. bdg.)
    D E F G H I J

Published in Canada by Greey de Pencier Books, Toronto
Canadian Cataloguing in Publication Data
Kassian, Olena.
Slip the otter finds a home
ISBN 0-919872-90-5
1. Otters – Juvenile fiction. I. Title.
PS8571.A77S44 1984   jC813'.54   C84-098450-2
PZ10.3.K37S1 1984

Slip the otter lived with her family
on a quiet river in a quiet forest.

There was lots to do
in Slip's home.

There were fat fish
to catch,

and crayfish to scoop off
the river bed.

Sometimes the otters
played hide and seek.

Other times, they wrestled with each other on the grassy banks.

For Slip, the best fun of all was gliding down
the long, slippery mud slide. Up she climbed
to the very top, and then SWOOSH
into the cool water with a great splash!

One day Slip could not find enough food to eat.
She became very hungry.

There was no longer enough food in the river for any of the otters. So they set off to look for a new place to live.

The new stream that the otters found was full of fish,
and it was beautiful, too. But Slip was too unhappy
to notice. She missed her favorite old spots.

Where would she play tag? Where would she play hide and seek?
How could she have any fun without a mud slide?

One day as Slip wandered around dragging her tail behind her she came upon a huge pile of sticks.

When she climbed to the top, she saw a lovely shimmering pond
on the other side. And there in the middle
was the strangest creature Slip had ever seen!

Down to the water she crept
to take a closer look.

What bright orange teeth!
What a funny flat tail!

It was a beaver pup
just about Slip's own age.

At first, the two animals swam around each other
slowly and carefully.

But before long, they were
playing tag together.

They even invented their own special game....

Slip chased after the beaver's tail and gave it a tug.

The beaver smacked a shower of water all over Slip!

When at last the new friends were hungry, the beaver headed straight for some green twigs to eat.

"Ugh!" thought Slip, "I'd much rather catch a fat crayfish."

Once Slip was full of food, she began to feel sleepy.
It had been a wonderful day, but it was time to return to her family.

Now that Slip had made a friend she felt much better about her new home.

She began to see some things she hadn't noticed before. Look, there were
some bullrushes for hide and seek and a waterfall for showering.
And there was one more surprise
waiting for Slip around the last bend in the stream.

There was the longest, curviest, most wonderful mud slide
she had ever seen! While Slip had been away,
her family had been busy making it.
Off she ran to take a ride.

It was a tired little Slip who curled up
in her dry, warm nest that night.

But how happy she was. This new home was as good
as her old home...and maybe even a little better.